This Walker book belongs to:

_____

_____

_____

For Daniel Goldin

First published 1997 by Walker Books Ltd
87 Vauxhall Walk, London SE11 5HJ

This edition published 2008

 20 19 18 17 16 15 14 13 12

This book has been typeset in Stempel Schneidler Medium

Printed in China

British Library Cataloguing in Publication Data:
a catalogue record for this book is available from the British Library

ISBN 978-1-4063-1357-4

www.walker.co.uk

Willy the Dreamer

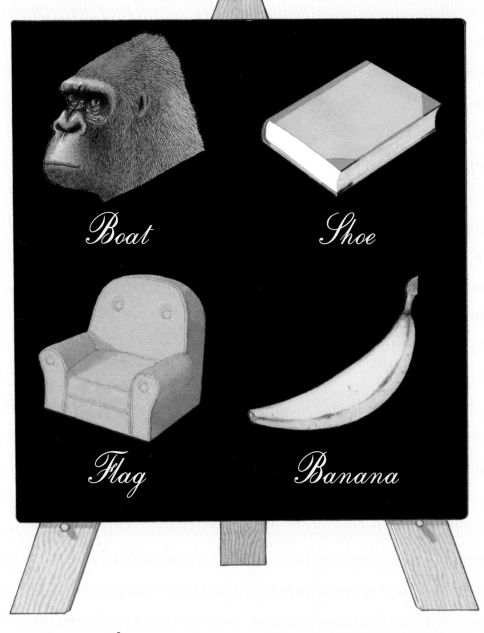

Boat

Shoe

Flag

Banana

Anthony Browne

WALKER BOOKS
AND SUBSIDIARIES
LONDON · BOSTON · SYDNEY · AUCKLAND

Willy dreams.

Sometimes Willy dreams that he's a film-star,

or a singer,

a sumo wrestler,

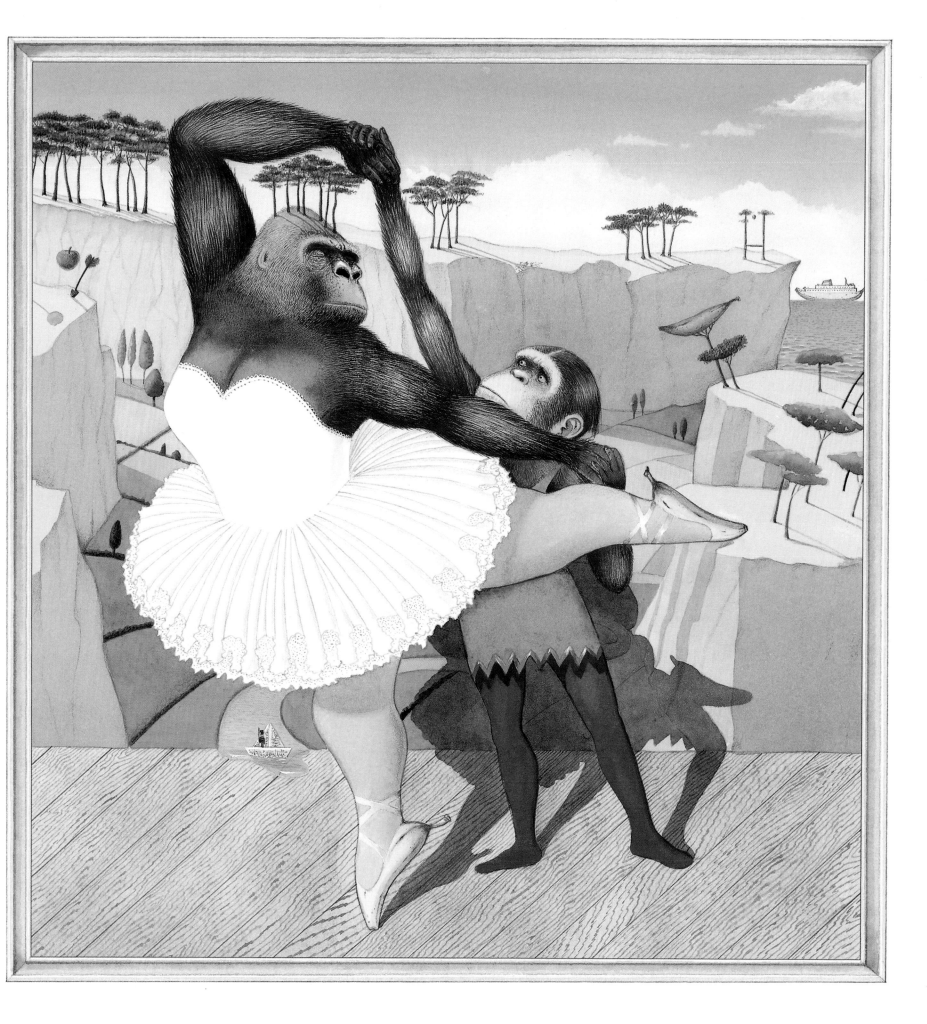

or a ballet dancer... Willy dreams.

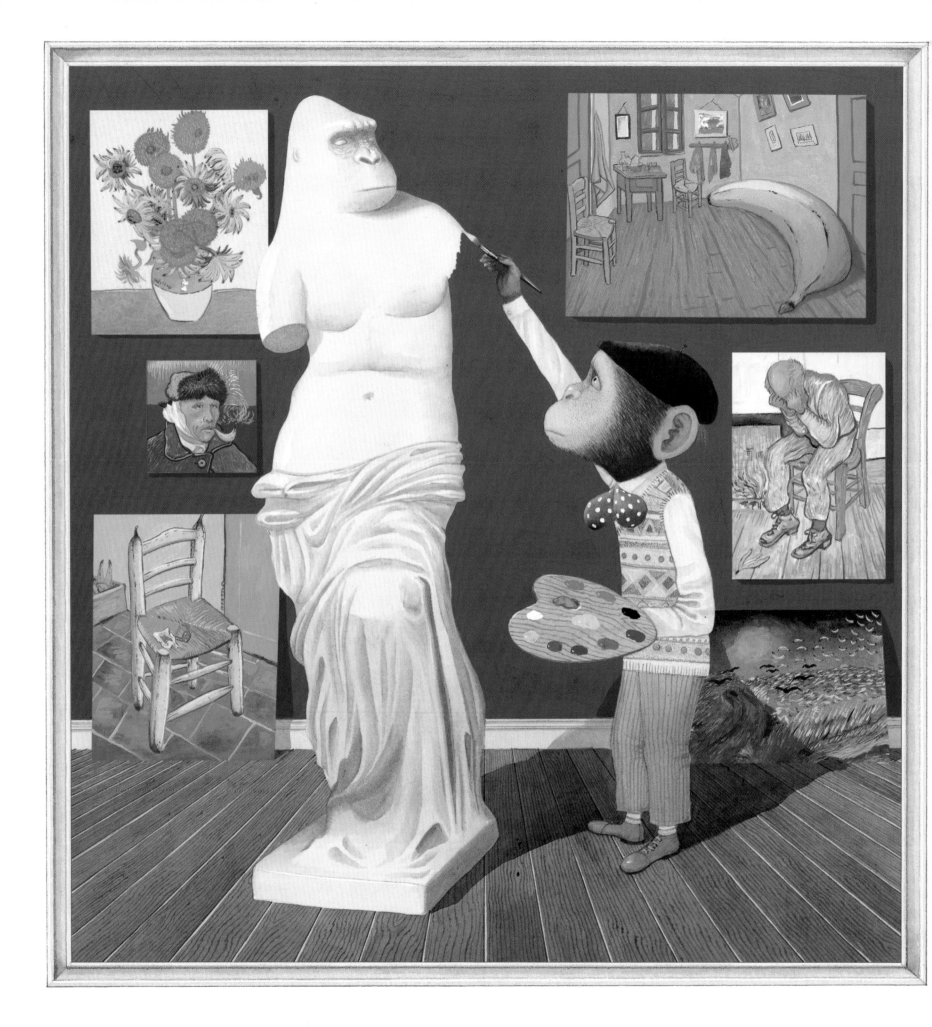

Sometimes Willy dreams that he's a painter,

or an explorer,

a famous writer,

or a scuba-diver... Willy dreams.

Sometimes Willy dreams that he can't run

but he can fly.

He's a giant,

or he's tiny... Willy dreams.

Sometimes Willy dreams that he's a beggar,

or a king.

He's in a strange landscape,

or all at sea... Willy dreams.

Sometimes Willy dreams of fierce monsters,

or super-heroes.

He dreams of the past ...

and, sometimes, the future.

Willy dreams.

Anthony Browne

Anthony Browne is one of the most celebrated author–illustrators of his generation. Acclaimed Children's Laureate from 2009 to 2011 and winner of multiple awards – including the prestigious Kate Greenaway Medal and the much coveted Hans Christian Andersen Award – Anthony is renowned for his unique style. His work is loved around the world.

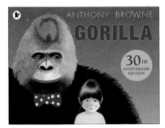

ISBN 978-1-4063-5233-7

ISBN 978-1-84428-559-4

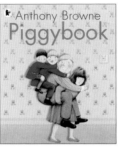

ISBN 978-1-4063-1328-4

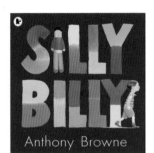

ISBN 978-1-4063-0576-0

ISBN 978-1-4063-1329-1

ISBN 978-1-4063-1930-9

ISBN 978-1-4063-1852-4

ISBN 978-0-7445-9858-2
ISBN 978-1-4063-2187-6
Board book edition

ISBN 978-1-4063-3851-5
ISBN 978-1-4063-4791-3
Board book edition

ISBN 978-0-7445-9857-5
ISBN 978-1-4063-2178-4
Board book edition

ISBN 978-1-4063-2625-3

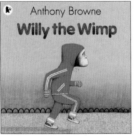

ISBN 978-1-4063-1874-6

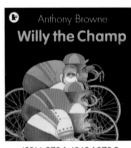

ISBN 978-1-4063-1873-9

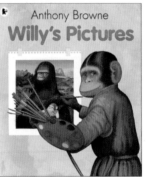

ISBN 978-1-4063-1356-7

ISBN 978-1-4063-1357-4

ISBN 978-1-4063-2628-4

ISBN 978-1-4063-3131-8

ISBN 978-1-4063-1339-0

ISBN 978-1-4063-4162-1

ISBN 978-1-4063-4163-8

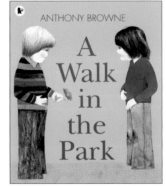

ISBN 978-1-4063-4164-5

Available from all good booksellers

www.walker.co.uk